Jean Nicolas Bouilly

L'Abbé de l'Epée

founder of the first institution in Paris for the deaf and dumb - a

dramatised tale founded on an historical fact

Jean Nicolas Bouilly

L'Abbé de l'Epée
founder of the first institution in Paris for the deaf and dumb - a dramatised tale
founded on an historical fact

ISBN/EAN: 9783337381929

Printed in Europe, USA, Canada, Australia, Japan

Cover: Foto ©Andreas Hilbeck / pixelio.de

More available books at **www.hansebooks.com**

L'ABBÉ DE L'EPÉE,

FOUNDER OF THE FIRST INSTITUTION IN PARIS
FOR THE DEAF AND DUMB.

A DRAMATISED TALE.

FOUNDED ON AN HISTORICAL FACT.

TRANSLATED FROM THE FRENCH OF J. N. BOUILLY,

BY

. . . . . . "Et ipse
" Notus in fratres animi paterni."
HORACE.

" Oh ! happiest who running o'er
With God's best gifts in mercy given,
Turn from their own abundant store
To teach the Dumb the songs of Heaven."

BRISTOL :
I. E. CHILLCOTT, 26, CLARE STREET.

LONDON :
HAMILTON, ADAMS, & CO. 32, PATERNOSTER ROW.

1870.

THE AUTHOR'S PREFACE.

(WRITTEN IN 1799.)

OF all my works, this has caused me the most labour and thought. I was long arrested by the part of the Deaf Mute, so difficult to portray on a large scale, and overcome all the difficulties it presented. I needed, indeed, the irresistible motive of doing honour to the memory of L'Abbé De l'Epée, the philanthropist, who devoted his time, strength, and fortune to give new life to that unfortunate class doomed apparently to perpetual nothingness; and who endeavoured to hide, under most touching modesty, the brilliancy of his genius and a combination of admirable virtues.

Two facts, related to me by persons who had the happiness of knowing him, will suffice to show the character of this great man.

L'Abbé De l'Epée had an income of about 14,000 francs: at his own expense he maintained his School for Deaf Mutes, allowing himself no more than 2000 francs for his personal expenses, regarding all the rest of his income as the patrimony of his pupils. In the severe winter of 1788, being then very old and attacked by many infirmities, he for some time denied himself a fire; his housekeeper divined his motive for this, and, at the head of forty Deaf Mutes who were in tears and making signs that he should take care of himself for their sake, she made him consent to exceed his usual expenses by about a hundred crowns; for this, however, the venerable old man never forgave himself, often telling his unfortunate children that he had wronged them in this instance.

In 1780 an ambassador from the Empress of Russia brought him her congratulations and a liberal donation. "Sir," said L'Abbé De l'Epée, " I never receive money : tell Her Majesty that if my labours have any claim to her favour, all I ask is, that she will send me a child born deaf and dumb."

Such devotion and greatness of soul could not fail to render the labours of this interpreter of Nature useful in a remarkable degree; indeed, she seems to have formed him to repair her wrongs, and thousands of blessings marked the career of this celebrated man.

The historical fact I retrace in this work excited the astonishment and admiration of all Europe, and I could not disguise from myself that my undertaking was a delicate one. I knew this memorable event had given rise to great judicial debates; I knew that power, intrigue, and above all, the hatred which the Archbishop of Paris then bore to L'Abbé De l'Epée, had prevented the latter from obtaining the reward of his long and patient toil. I knew, besides, that people had gone so far as to calumniate this venerable man, and even to spread the report that he repented of what he had done for his pupil. I employed, therefore, all the means dictated by delicacy, not to awaken quarrels and excite resentment; but, limiting myself to the principal fact, and adding incidental developments and fictitious personages, I gave myself up with security to all the flights of imagination, which pure zeal animated and discretion restrained.

However, in spite of all these precautions on which I prided myself, and which many men, in my place, might not have troubled themselves about, I learn that at the very moment in which I am writing this Preface, people whom I have never seen, and whose very existence I was ignorant of, are taking proceedings, amongst the higher powers, to stop the representation of my Play. I am accused also in the papers of having brought it out only to trouble their peace and compromise their honour. These charges are too ill-founded for me to undertake to contradict them; but it will never be believed that the author of L'Abbé De l'Epée had, in composing his work, base and perfidious intentions. The numerous spectators who, at every representation of my Play, honour me with their applause, are a guarantee for this.

That the pupil of L'Abbé De l'Epée was recognized Count of Solar by the decree of the Châtelet de Paris, June 8th, 1781; that this same decree was nullified in 1792, is of little consequence to me. It is not the less true that the great man I write of succeeded in making an interesting member of society of a young Deaf Mute (whom I call Julius Harancour); that he, with this unsupported orphan, succeeded after great difficulty in discovering his native place, and that far from regretting what he had done for his pupil, L'Abbé De l'Epée died with the firm conviction that this unfortunate man belonged to an honourable family, and that he had been the victim of most criminal cupidity. I have been assured of this by several persons who knew the Founder of the Institution for the Deaf and Dumb. This I have wished to commemorate in order that his memory may be honoured, and an interest created in favour of those whom he made the legatees of his genius. I have had the happiness of achieving this double aim. All eyes are moistened with sweet tears at seeing on the French Stage, L'Abbé De l'Epée,—and the proscription of the good, the respectable Sicard has at length ceased ! Though the supporters of calumny unite and redouble their efforts, they can never tear from me the pure joy I have already derived from my work.

J. N. BOUILLY.

THE CHARACTERS AND COSTUMES.

L'Abbé De l'Epée: Founder of the Institution for Deaf
Mutes; age 66.—Brown coat, with black waistcoat,
knee-breeches and stockings; white hair, cut round, and
curling slightly at the ends; small cap, white collar,
clerical hat. On his first entrance he has grey cloth
gaiters, with small black buttons; his shoes covered
with dust, and a knotted stick in his hand. Afterwards,
black stockings and clean square-toed shoes, with small
silver buckles. He maintains a simple, patriarchal
character, with a penetration which nothing escapes;
while genius and goodness, with the tone of good society
and amiable manners, are displayed by turns; but above
all, gentle, unaffected piety, and an unbounded trust in
God, to Whom he attributes his success, and devotes all
his labours. He is firm, without arrogance in his
treatment of the man who wronged his pupil, and he
shows a perfect knowledge of Nature.

Theodore or Julius: the only scion of the Earls of Harancour; born Deaf and Dumb; age 18.—Nut-coloured
great coat, not wrapping over; white waistcoat, grey
breeches, any coloured stockings; small boots, in buskin
fashion; coloured cravat, loosely tied; hair slightly
powdered; round hat, which he throws off on entering,
and thus shows all the expression of his face. Boots
covered with dust on his first appearance. He shows
great intelligence, and extreme sensibility; unreserved
confidence in his tutor; and, with a quiet, modest de-
meanour, the desire of creating an interest in his fate.
His glance is quick and penetrating, always accompanied
by a gesture signifying that he understands or sees or
wishes something to be explained. But the continual
proof of his deafness is a happy, amiable smile, when
people about him are moved to commiseration by his
affliction and misfortunes.

Darlemont: uncle and despoiler of the young Count; age
55.—Dress of a rich financier; wig, round and powdered.
This very important though odious character wears a
gloomy and rapid glance, but the exterior of dignity does
not allow remorse to appear.

St. Alme: Darlemont's only son, companion of Julius in
childhood; age 20.—In the First Act, plain frock coat,
no hat; afterwards, always, coat embroidered in the

highest fashion, sword and plumed hat; of ardent temper, unconquerable love, and sensitiveness even to a fault. In the Fourth and Fifth Acts the honour and fate of his father supersede love.

FRANVAL: a celebrated Counsellor at Toulouse; age about 40.—In the Second Act, silk dressing-gown and slippers; black breeches, waistcoat, and stockings; hair dressed and powdered, raised on a comb. Afterwards, plain black suit, natural long hair, hat under his arm. The enemy of presumption and friend to good breeding,—every step, every movement is easy though dignified. He carries the love of great men to enthusiasm. He neglects nothing which contributes to the happiness of others, especially his sister; but his character is chiefly marked by the painful struggle between his friendship for St. Alme and admiration for De l'Epée.

MRS. FRANVAL: mother of Franval and Clemence; the widow of a Senator; age about 60.—Dress, heavy material, full and plaited; dress-cap, neck well covered. Of noble though bitter temperament; increasing amiability towards the end.

CLEMENCE: age 18.—Hair simply dressed; white robe; modest ingenuousness; concealed love. In the Fifth Act she is full of expressive, pantomimic gestures.

DUPRÉ: an old Footman of the Harancour family, but now in the service of Darlemont, whose accomplice he is; age 60. — White bag-wig, coat, waistcoat, breeches, and stockings, all of a brownish colour. Sensitive, energetic; face full of remorse.

DUBOIS: Darlemont's Footman; age 35.—Livery, laced hat.

DOMINIC: an old Servant in the Franval family; age 66.— White bag-wig; coat and breeches, iron-grey, with plain silver button-holes; waistcoat, scarlet and laced; no hat; stockings rolled round; shoes, square toes. A merry temper, jocose and familiar, fond of watching and teasing the lovers; inquisitive and chatty in ordinary matters, civil and discreet in serious affairs.

MARIANNE: widow of an old Porter in the Harancour House; age 60.—Poorly clad, boots turning up at the toes, large cap, black head-dress, tied in a knot under the chin; a good and grateful nurse.

SCENE: THROUGHOUT AT TOULOUSE.

ACT I.

SCENE.—*A Public Square in the City of Toulouse; on the left, the front entrance of the Old Mansion of the Harancour Family; opposite, the Franvals' House.*

(ST. ALME, in morning dress, comes out of the mansion alone; stands motionless in the centre, his eyes fixed on one of the windows in the Franvals' House. Dubois follows him an instant later.)

DUBOIS. Who would have thought, Sir, of your being out already? (Aside) He doesn't hear me; he's quite, entirely,—there's no head when you're in love; you see everything, and yet nothing; you hear everything, and say nothing.

ST. ALME (rousing from his reverie, and seeing him). Ah! you here, Dubois?

DUBOIS. I looked for you, in vain, in your room.

ST. A. What do you want with me?

DUBOIS. To tell you, Sir, about the conversation you wished me to have with Dupré.

ST. A. Have you made him explain my father's intentions? He is his sole confidante.

DUBOIS. That is true. There never was a valet who knew so much of his master's secrets.

ST. A. Well?

DUBOIS. Well, Sir, I have executed your orders, and learnt all.

ST. A. (quickly). My father, doubtless——.

DUBOIS. He's a rough one to handle, is that good Dupré.

ST. A. What's that to me? Tell me only——.

DUBOIS. With all that he has a sadness, a dreaminess, one would think he bears about the remembrance of a bad action.

ST. A. He! Why, he's the most honest man! Ever since he has been in my father's service,—but to the fact, I command you.

DUBOIS. You must know, then, that last night

when everybody in the house had retired, I went to Dupré, pretending I wanted a light, and then I made the conversation turn upon the plans for your establishment, and found that your fears were but too well grounded, your father having already given orders for your marriage with the daughter of President Argental.

St. A. Heavens! How unfortunate!

Dubois. The young lady is not pretty,—no, she is not pretty,—but she is the only daughter of the first magistrate in Toulouse, and heiress of an immense fortune.

St. A. What is her father's rank to me! and what are her riches to me! All, together, are not worth one look from Clemence!

Dubois. True, Miss Clemence is charming; but, Sir, your father will never consent to her being your wife.

St. A. How! Why? Is she not the daughter of a magistrate whose memory is still revered; the sister of the most celebrated counsellor in Toulouse, whom I have the happiness of calling my friend? Formerly, my father, a merchant, of the middle rank, would have thought it a great honour for me to be united to the daughter of the Senator Franval; but since he has possessed the wealth of young Harancour, whose uncle and guardian he was, his soul is given up to ambition.

Dubois. I have often heard young Count Harancour spoken of by the old servants; was he not born deaf and dumb?

St. A. Yes; and my father took him to Paris about eight years ago, to consult the doctors as to his infirmity; but whether the remedies administered were beyond his strength, or that nature was exhausted, he died there in the arms of Dupré, who alone had accompanied my father.

Dubois. Then no wonder I so often surprise Dupré, with his eyes fixed on the portrait of that child, among the family pictures in the drawing-room.

St. A. (with emotion). It is natural; the young Count was the only scion of an illustrious family, of whom Dupré was long the faithful servant. My poor little Julius! How we loved each other! and I owe my life to him. How courageously he exposed his own for me! Never, never shall I cease to love him! He was nearly ten years old, and I about twelve, when we were separated. I well remember the moment of his departure; the unhappy boy could not speak, but his face was so expressive, all his movements were so marked—he embraced me so tenderly,—one might have thought he had a presentiment it was for the last time. Ah! why is he not still alive! I should have one friend more; and my father, less opulent, would not now oppose my being the husband of Clemence.

Dubois. Doubtless, Sir, you are quite sure that the young lady returns your love?

St. A. You well know I go every morning to her brother's rooms to perfect my study of the law. Clemence never fails to join us there, under a thousand ingenious pretexts which love alone could inspire. If our eyes meet, she blushes and her breath is short; if she speaks to me her voice falters, her lips tremble, as though she feared some secret might escape. If all this be not love, by what stronger proofs, or more certain signs can it be known?

Dubois. I will venture, nevertheless, to observe, Sir, that before undertaking anything, you should have the formal avowal of the lady and the consent of her family.

St. A. I am sure, beforehand, of her brother's. Franval is too penetrating not to have discovered that I adore Clemence; and if he did not approve of my love for his sister, would he lavish such care on me? would he receive me with such kindness? All I fear is her mother's temper.

Dubois. The dear lady is rather blunt and cross.

St. A. Mrs. Franval, of high birth, is much prouder even than my father; but her son's influence may easily remove all objections, and make her sanction my love.

(The door of Franval's house opens and Dominic appears.)

Dubois (speaking while Dominic is shutting the door). Here comes their old man-servant; let us make him talk, it will not be difficult. Let us try, especially to make ourselves doubly sure of the young lady's feelings.

Dominic (merry and chatty). Oh! Oh! I did not expect to find you here so early. Good morning, neighbour (to Dubois, shaking hands with him). (To St. A.) It is true that the morning air cools the blood, calms the mind, and at your age—(he titters).—Besides, as the proverb says, "Love and Rest don't dwell easily together."

Dubois. How! what do you mean, Dominic?

Dominic (tittering). Come, come; you, with your hypocritical look!—Oh! I have good eyes, and in spite of my sixty years I feel strong enough still to defy the most cunning lover to make me lose the track. (Then to St. A. who is still looking up at the windows.) You expect to see some one at the window? We do not appear so early. We were up till two o'clock this morning practising on the guitar the pretty verses you made on our convalescence, and we are now asleep, dreaming probably of the author. Ha! ha! ha! ha!

St. A. Your mirth disarms me, good Dominic, and makes me banish all subterfuge. Yes, I do adore your lovely mistress.

Dubois. And it is precisely of that love I wish to cure my master.

Dominic. Cure him of it! Why?

Dubois. You, with so much experience, Dominic, must have remarked, as I have, that Miss Franval is far from sharing the sentiments with which she has inspired my master.

Dominic (ironically). Ah! you have remarked that?

DUBOIS. Decidedly. It is very evident.

DOMINIC (in the same tone). Well, you are very acute. Tut, tut! What a wiseacre for reading people!

ST. A. Have you observed on the contrary—

DOMINIC. That my young lady loves you—what do I say?—loves you? That is nothing, Sir, —she thinks only, acts only, exists only for you.

ST. A. (with joy). What? Can it be—

DUBOIS (aside, restraining him). Be calm, if you wish to know all. (Aloud.) But in fact, Dominic, what proofs have you that her love—

DOMINIC. What proofs?—a thousand,—if it were only in the illness we thought would have carried her off a few months ago. In her delirium who did she call every minute? Mr. St. Alme. When reading the list of the names of people who came to enquire after her health, at whose name did she stop and blush? At that of Mr. St. Alme. (Imitating the weak voice of a convalescent lady), "He has been, then?" said she to me with that angel-voice you know so well. "Yes, Miss." "Often?" "Every hour." "And he showed—?" "Oh! the greatest interest, the tenderest anxiety." I saw her poor weak limbs tremble, and her lovely eyes moistened with sweet tears, while her pretty mouth, where her sweet smile appeared again, let these words escape: "I am better, much better; I feel I am restored to life"—(tittering). Ha! ha! ha! ha!

ST. A. (with difficulty restraining his emotion) Certainly all these circumstances—

DUBOIS (bluntly). Are not sufficient, in my opinion, Sir, to satisfy you.

DOMINIC. Hey? not sufficient? And then that dispute I had with her the other day (laughing heartily), ha! ha!—I cannot help laughing at it still!

ST. A. Well, what was it?

DOMINIC. I went, as usual, to arrange her room. She was busy finishing a miniature likeness, working so intently that she paid no more attention to me than if I had been a hundred miles off. Well, I approached her gently—nothing amuses me so much as watching—lovers,—

St. A. Well?

Dominic. I cast my eyes on the portrait and recognised you.

St. A. (in transports). 'Twas I?

Dominic. Yourself. "Oh! how like it is!" cried I, involuntarily. "Do you think so?" said she, frightened, immediately giving up work. "One must be blind, Miss, not to see that is——" "Who, then?" "Why, Mr. St. Alme, certainly." "Mr. St. Alme," replied she, embarrassed and vexed,—"it is not he; it is my brother, whom I wished to paint from memory." "That may be, Miss; but, without doubt, you mistook one for the other, for I assure you it is as like Mr. St. Alme as like can be." "And I tell you it is my brother, it can be nobody but my brother." And thereupon she hid the portrait in her bosom, and went away, angry with me for the first time in her life. —Ha! ha! ha! ha!

St. A. How precious these details are to me!

Dominic. But talking with you I am forgetting—

St. A. (detaining him) One moment, good Dominic, one moment! You cannot imagine the good you are doing me!

Dominic. Indeed, I believe that; but you cannot imagine either the commissions I am loaded with. It is my mistress here, and my master there, and above all my young lady. But, Sir, take particular care that you do not allow her to suspect we have been talking together; for she would scold me roundly! Besides, young people, you see, have a way of loving—a dissimulation (pressing Dubois' hand); good bye, you clever fellow, you clear-sighted observer. Will you say now that your master is not beloved, that you have remarked it very decidedly, that it is very evident? Ha! ha! (Exit, laughing heartily).

St. A. Well, Dubois?

Dubois. Well, Sir, your love is most tenderly returned; nothing can be clearer.

St. A. And they will marry me to another than Clemence! Never! never!

Dubois. In that case you must immediately think of the means of putting a stop to your father's plans; he is imperious and violent. I caution you, for the crisis will be terrible.

St. A. You must help me in this great affair.

Dubois. Take my advice, then. First, go at your usual hour to Mr. Franval; tell him of your love for his sister, and of your resolution to make her your wife; then declare your feelings to the young lady herself in the presence of her brother; obtain their consent, and go at once to the house of President Argental, whose daughter you are intended to marry; interest him in your own natural, frank way, and thus destroy in their very source your father's intentions.

St. A. You are right. I will adopt this plan. It is a delicate affair, no doubt,—but, with respect and candour—the President is just and sensible; he will sympathize with my troubles, and take an interest in my love. His house is not two steps off; go and enquire at what hour he can grant me a private interview; then come and help me to dress.

Dubois. I will return immediately. (Exit.)

(St. Alme re-enters his house. Dubois goes off on one side, as De l'Epée and Theodore appear on the other. They observe everything, Theodore preceding De l'Epée in the greatest excitement. Their shoes are covered with dust, and they look like people just arrived from a long journey. The old man has a knotty stick in his hand. Theodore makes signs that he recognizes the Square they are entering.)

De l'Epée. By this sudden agitation, this

change depicted in his face, I can no longer doubt that he recognizes these objects.

THEODORE signs more expressively that he remembers the spot.

DE L'EPÉE. Can it be that we have at length come to the end of our long and painful search?

THEODORE looks fixedly at the Harancour's house, advances several steps towards the door, utters a cry, and returns breathless to the arms of De l'Epée.

DE L'EPÉE. What a piercing cry! He scarcely breathes! I never saw him so agitated!

THEODORE makes rapid signs, announcing that he has found his father's home. He lays his hands one over the other, building up as it were, and joins them together with straightened fingers in the form of a roof—then designates with his right hand the height of a child, about two feet high.

DE L'EPÉE (pointing to the mansion). Yes, 'tis there he was born. The dwelling which saw our birth—the beloved scenes of our childhood, never lose their power over us!

THEODORE makes signs expressing gratitude to De l'Epée, whose hand he kisses.

DE L'EPÉE signs that it is not he whom he must thank, but God alone, who has directed their search. Theodore immediately falls on one knee, and expresses by signs that he is praying heaven to shed blessings on his benefactor. De l'Epée bends with uncovered head, and offers up the following prayer :—

O Thou, who dost order, as Thou wilt, the actions of men, Thou who didst inspire me to undertake this great work, God Almighty, accept my thanks, and the thanks of this orphan, of whom Thou hast made me the second father —our thanks for Thy protection and guidance hitherto. If I have worthily fulfilled my duty, if my devoted labours have found grace in Thy sight, let the reward be upon this unfortunate youth—suffer me to find mine in his happiness.

(They rise, and fall into each other's arms.)

Now let us enquire to whom this mansion belongs.

He makes signs to Theodore, who wishes to enter the house ; he holds him back, and expresses by pantomime, a young man presenting himself, and driven away without being listened to. Theodore expresses in his turn that he understands De l'Epée, and yields to his advice.

(Enter Dubois, by the same way he had gone out).

DE L'EPÉE (aside). Here is some one who may be able to inform me. (After making a sign to Theodore to control himself, he addresses Dubois.) Can you tell me the name of this Square ?

DUBOIS (aside, examining them). These gentlemen, it strikes me, are strangers. You are in St. George's Square.

DE L'EPÉE. I am obliged to you (detains Dubois who was going away). One question more, I beg you. Do you know this large house ?

DUBOIS. Do I know it ? I have lived there five years.

DE L'EPÉE. I could not, then, address a better person. You call it——?

DUBOIS. It is the old family mansion of the Harancours.

DE L'EPÉE. The Harancours ! (very marked manner.)

DUBOIS. At the present time it belongs to Mr. Darlemont, in whose service I am.

THEODORE, during this dialogue, goes to look again at the house very attentively, and leans against the door with joy and emotion.

DE L'EPÉE. And what is this Mr. Darlemont ?

DUBOIS (aside). Plenty of questions ! What is he ?

DE L'EPÉE. Yes. His rank ? His profession ?

DUBOIS. His profession ? I don't know that he has any, unless it be that he is one of the richest men in Toulouse.—But I am wanted,— you must excuse—.

DE L'EPÉE. I should be sorry to detain you a moment from your business.

B

Dubois (aside, going away). These strangers are very inquisitive !

(He re-enters the mansion.)

De l'Epée (looking after him). He little knows what urged me to ask him those questions ! We must not lose a single instant, and first we must find a safe hotel. This mansion which belongs, doubtless, to an ancient family in this great city, this Darlemont who is its present possessor; all this must be well known in Toulouse. Let us make all proper enquiries. (Pressing Theodore in his arms, who has come back to him enquiringly.) If Theodore belong to sensible parents, they are certainly still lamenting his loss. What joy I shall have in restoring him to their arms. If he be the victim of wicked men, grant, O God, that I may unmask and confound them, to prove that there is no crime which Thou dost not bring to light, and that none escapes Thy eternal justice.

(He leads Theodore off, both making signs—the latter looking back several times at the mansion)

The Curtain falls.

End of Act I.

ACT II.

Franval's Study.—*On the left hand a business writing-table, on which stands a vase of flowers. Here and there are books, maps, and files of papers.*

(Franval, alone in dressing-gown and slippers, seated at his writing-table, and holding several papers in his hand.)

This affair, of which I am the sole arbitrator, is never out of my head for an instant. There is nothing more important for society, nothing more honourable for my profession ; this re-uniting of a separated man and wife. Alas ! there are but too many such cases ! O my times ! O my country! I will stand up against this abuse which defiles and ruins you. I will expose the very depths of the abyss. Should selfishness and false philosophy oppose me, I shall have the wails of outraged nature,——I shall have the sad spectacle of thousands of deserted children, and the patriarchal cry of all the heads of families on my side to withstand them.

(Enter Clemence, simply dressed, though with taste; she carries in her hand a wicker-basket full of flowers.)

CLEMENCE. Good morning, brother.

FRANVAL. Good morning, Clemence. (They kiss each other.)

CLEMENCE. I am come to renew the flowers on your table. (She takes out those in the vase, and substitutes fresh ones from the basket.)

FRANVAL. How can I help being happy? Every morning fresh flowers and a kiss from my lovely sister! (Smiling.) I know a young lawyer to whom this would be at least as beneficial as to me.

CLEMENCE (in confusion). Who do you mean, brother?

FRANVAL. Who? Don't blush like that, now. (He rises, takes her by the hand, and leads her forward, looking fixedly at her.) Clemence?

CLEMENCE (casting down her eyes). Brother!

FRANVAL. These flowers are very sweet to me —your kisses very dear; but all this would have no charm for me if you did not add still—

CLEMENCE. What?

FRANVAL. Your confidence,—but my dear sister, your mind is too pure not to be easily read—

CLEMENCE. Oh! say no more!

FRANVAL. And why deny yourself so true a feeling? Does not St. Alme possess every quality which renders him worthy of your love?

CLEMENCE (with ingenuousness). That is just what I think.

FRANVAL. I will not speak of his face—

CLEMENCE. How expressive it is!

FRANVAL. Or his manner.

CLEMENCE. How noble and modest he is!

FRANVAL. I will dwell only on his character. What temper can be more frank, more amiable than his? What mortal ever offered a surer presage of happiness for a wife?

CLEMENCE. I have often said that to myself.

FRANVAL. In a word, he loves you.

CLEMENCE. Do you think so?

FRANVAL. You have not perceived it?

CLEMENCE. I have been afraid of deceiving myself.

FRANVAL. You confess, then, that he is dear to you?

CLEMENCE. Ah! brother, brother, you have torn my secret from me. (She throws herself on his breast.)

Enter St. Alme, richly dressed.

ST. ALME (to Franval, pressing his hand). Good morning, my friend. (To Clemence, with much emotion.) Miss Clemence, good morning.

FRANVAL (gaily). How you are decked out this morning! This full-dress announces some great project.

ST. ALME (with irritation). I never had a more important one.

FRANVAL (seriously). What is the matter?

CLEMENCE. You are disturbed.

ST. ALME. Who would not be disturbed in my place. I am in despair.

CLEMENCE. Heavens!

ST. ALME (to Franval). My friend, I never stood in greater need of you.

FRANVAL. Explain yourself, St. Alme.

CLEMENCE. I am in your way, perhaps. (Going.)

ST. ALME (detaining her). No, no, stay; pray stay. I have just had a scene with my father.

FRANVAL. How? What?

ST. ALME. The horrible threats with which he has overwhelmed me have struck me to the heart. And why? Because I cannot satisfy his ambition. If only my blood, my life, could do it, I would

give them up without regret—, but to renounce
for ever all that I love, to forget—

FRANVAL. Be calm, my friend, and tell me all.

ST. ALME. It is on the subject of that marriage
which I feared, and which I have mentioned to
you several times. My father has just now signi-
fied to me his intention that within three days it
shall be concluded. "In three days! No! Never!"
At these words which forcibly escaped me, my
father flew into a passion, which neither my
apologies or entreaties could pacify. . . . At
length, compelled to explain myself, and hoping
that the name of her whom I adore would disarm
him, I confessed that my heart had made its choice,
and mentioned Clemence.

CLEMENCE. Who? Me?

ST. ALME (sinking on one knee). It is no longer
possible to hide it from you. Yes, 'tis you, you
only, whom I love, whom I shall ever love—
and if you approve,——

CLEMENCE (in the greatest agitation, and raising
St. Alme). Upon this confession, what did your
father say?

ST. ALME. "Yes, she is beautiful," said he,
in a confused and embarrassed voice, "Yes, she
is worthy of your choice, but I have disposed of
you—you must forget her." "It is impossible."
"Impossible!" replied he in a terrific voice, and
then giving full vent to his anger, he reproached
me most bitterly, threatened me with his malediction, and commanded me to quit his presence for
ever. At this frightful order my blood boiled, my
brain reeled; I feared I should lose my senses:
and to be able to bear the idea of banishment from
my father, I take refuge with my friend.

FRANVAL. And your friend makes it his duty
to help you with his advice;—the first I give you,
St. Alme, is to moderate your feelings which dis-
tract you, and remember that a father is to be
respected, even in his errors.

St. Alme. Clemence never was dearer to me, and if you both consent—

Franval. I should have been happy, doubtless, to have seen you the husband of my sister, and to have blended the names of brother and friend,—Clemence herself—

Clemence. Brother!

Franval. And why refuse him an avowal which alone can soften his grief? Yes, St. Alme, whatever may be your feelings for Clemence, they are only in exchange for those you have inspired her with.

St. Alme. It is true, then! I am beloved! (To Clemence) Ah, to believe so much happiness I must hear it confirmed by you.

Clemence. Since my brother has told all—it is no longer possible for me to be silent.—Yes, you are dear to me; oh! very dear!—But why reveal the secret of my heart when your father opposes—

St. Alme (overjoyed). I shall be able to soften him,—to overcome his inflexibility in spite of himself. Ah! if, before this confession, I resisted the wrath of a father, with what power shall I not resist it now? To all his remarks, to all his rage, I shall only reply, "Clemence loves me, father; Clemence loves me!"—But I am forgetting that I must go to President Argental—he can, more than anyone, second my plans,—I will move him, I will touch his heart.—Ah! who would not be interested in him who, like me, can say, "Clemence loves me!"—(He kisses her hands several times, and goes out quickly.)

Franval. What is he going to do at the house of the president? What is his design?

Clemence. I fear very much that his extreme excitement may lead him to commit some imprudence. *(Enter Dominic, with several large books under his arm.)*

Dominic. My Mistress desires to know if breakfast may be in your study to-day.

Franval. Certainly.

CLEMENCE. You have not yet seen her this morning, brother; you know how much she thinks of all these attentions.

FRANVAL. I have had so many engagements. I will go to her room, and give her my arm down stairs.

CLEMENCE. And I will run and prepare breakfast.

(They go out separately.)

DOMINIC (alone; after having placed the books on the writing-table). Ouf!—If I have not walked two leagues in Toulouse this monring, my name is not Dominic. Let me see if I have executed all my commissions, (he takes a little memorandum out of his pocket) for my mistress will be sure to say, "Ah! now! How tiresome that old man is! He has no memory!" (He reads:) go first to the house of the Lady President Arbancas, and to the Prior of St. Mark's, to invite them.—I have done all that. Then go to my master's librarian for the books.—Here they are (pointing to the books he has laid on the table). Come back from there to the house of Bailiff Prestolet, to tell him that he may give up his proceedings against the incendiaries in the suburb, and that they are ready to pay the six hundred pounds in question.—Ah! It is my master, the Counsellor, who furnishes the sum in secret, to save that wretched family. (Reading again:) then go down St. Lawrence Street, and give £2 from Miss Clemence to the widow of the old porter of the Harancour House. Poor dear woman, how she did bless the young lady! It is true that she forestalls all her wants, and with such discretion, such delicacy!—But here comes some one, I must make haste.

(He brings forward a little round table, with a marble top.)

(Enter FRANVAL, Mrs. FRANVAL, and CLEMENCE. Dominic fetches a tray on which is everything necessary for breakfast, places it on the table, and exit.)

Mrs. FRANVAL (leaning on the arm of her son). Yes, my son, there are few families in Toulouse which bear a more ancient name than yours. I hope you will always show yourself worthy of it, though you are only a Counsellor.

FRANVAL. My profession, mother, confers honour upon him who practises it,—whatever he may be.

(They seat themselves at the table : Clemence makes breakfast.)

Mrs. FRANVAL. It is terrible to me, I cannot disguise it, not to see you a Senator, like your ancestors. But misfortunes and the injustice of men compelled me to sell that post on the death of your father.

FRANVAL. And thus made me acquire by talent, the consideration which I should have obtained only by prejudice and chance.

Mrs. FRANVAL. I know full well that you hold one of the first places at the bar; but it is still derogatory, my son, still derogatory.

(Dominic brings a basket of fruit and some rolls, which he places on the table, and a letter which he gives to Mrs. F.)

DOMINIC. Here is a letter which Mr. Darlemont's footman has just brought for you, Madam.

FRANVAL (in a marked tone). From Mr. Darlemont ?

Mrs. F. (opening the letter). What does that man want with me ?—(she takes her glasses and reads.) "Madam, allow me to address myself to you, in order to uphold my most sacred rights." What does he mean ? (To Dominic.) Leave us.

(Exit Dominic.)

(Continuing to read) "To uphold my most sacred rights. My son loves your daughter, and declares that his love is returned." (Clemence starts, Mrs. F. lookes severely at her.)

FRANVAL. Mother, read on, I beg you.

Mrs. F. (reading). "Whatever the love of my son may be, how lawfully soever he may have fixed his choice upon Miss Franval, their union cannot take place." (Vehemently.) No, indeed, it never shall take place !

CLEMENCE (aside). How I suffer!

FRANVAL (to his mother). Pray, finish.

Mrs. F. (reading). "I hope, therefore, Madam, that you will no longer admit him at your house, nor aid him in braving the rights and authority of a father.—DARLEMONT." "That you will no longer aid him!" Never was there such disrespect, such audacity!

FRANVAL. Mother, be calm.

Mrs. F. Hey? Who told this little merchant, grown into a great lord, that I was seeking to ally myself with him? Has he forgotten that, in spite of all his riches, there is between us such disproportion of birth,—I hope, my son, that after this insult, you will no longer receive young St. Alme here; and, as to his father, if ever—

(Enter Dominic.)

DOMINIC. Sir, there is a stranger who wishes to speak to you.

FRANVAL. A stranger?

DOMINIC. He is an old man with white hair— he looks like an old clergyman.

FRANVAL. Show him in. (Exit Dominic.)

(Franval rises, and wheels the little table aside.)

Mrs. F. (still seated and reading the letter over again angrily). "Their union cannot take place."

CLEMENCE (aside to Franval). Oh, Brother! no more happiness for me!

DOMINIC. Come in, Sir, come in. (On entering, De l'Epée bows to Mrs. Franval and Clemence, who bow in return.)

DE L'EPÉE (to Franval, advancing to meet him). Have I the honour of speaking to Mr. Franval?

FRANVAL. I am Mr. Franval, Sir.

DE L'EPÉE. Can you grant me a few minutes conversation?

FRANVAL. Willingly. (He makes a sign to Dominic to go. Exit Dominic.) May I ask whom I have the honour of receiving in my house?

DE LEpée. I come from Paris: my name is De l'Epée.

FRANVAL. De l'Epée! The Founder of the Institution for the Deaf and Dumb?

DE L'EPÉE. I am he.

FRANVAL. Mother! Sister! You see one of the men who do honour to our age.

(Mrs. Franval and Clemence rise and courtesy with much respect to De l'Epée.)

DE L'EPÉE (modestly). Sir,—

FRANVAL. I often read of the miraculous results of your teaching, and every time with more surprise and admiration! Believe me, nobody feels more interest in your labours, or more respect for your name than myself.

DE L'EPÉE. I see I have done well in coming to you.

FRANVAL. To what do I owe the happiness of seeing you?

DE L'EPÉE. To your reputation, Sir, for you also are widely known. I wish to communicate to you an affair of the highest importance.

Mrs. F. (to Clemence). Let us retire, my dear, and leave these gentlemen.

DE L'EPÉE. What I have to reveal cannot be too much known. I desire, especially, to interest sensitive minds. If these ladies will listen to me—

Mrs. F. (with some curiosity). Since you allow us—

CLEMENCE (aside, and looking earnestly at De l'Epée). What a fatherly voice! What a venerable appearance!

FRANVAL (offering an easy chair to De l'Epée). Sit down, pray.

(He seats himself between Franval and Mrs. F.; Clemence takes a seat near her mother.)

DE L'EPÉE. This is the subject which brings me here.—I shall be rather tedious, perhaps; but I must neglect nothing to attain the end I aim at.

FRANVAL (eagerly). We are listening to you.

DE L'EPÉE. About eight years ago, towards the end of autumn, a police officer brought to my house at Paris a young Deaf-mute, whom the watch

had found on the Pont-Neuf early in the night.
I examined the child, he seemed about nine or ten
years old, and had an interesting face. The coarse
clothes he wore, made me think at first that he
belonged to the poorer classes, and I promised to
take charge of him. The next day, examining
him more attentively, I remarked pride in his
looks, and surprise at finding himself covered with
rags ; and I surmised he was a disguised child, wil-
fully deserted. I had him advertised in the public
papers, I described his appearance, and gave all
necessary information, but in vain. It is not the
afflicted who are eagerly sought for and claimed.
Finding my search useless, and convinced that
this child was the victim of some secret intrigue, I
thought no longer of gaining information from anyone but himself. I gave him the adopted name of
Theodore, and placed him in my school, where he
soon distinguished himself : he confirmed my
hopes so well that, at the end of three years, his
mind opened, naturally, and he found a new life.
A thousand remembrances then flashed upon him.
I spoke to him by signs as quick as thought, and
he answered in the same way. One day as we
were walking in Paris in front of the Palais de
Justice, on seeing a magistrate alight from his
carriage, he started. I asked him what caused
that involuntary movement. He made me understand that a man dressed also in purple and
ermine had often pressed him in his arms and shed
tears over him. By this I supposed that he was
the son or near relative of a magistrate ; that this
magistrate, from his robes, could belong only to
the highest post, and consequently that the native
place of my pupil was a capital city. Another
day, walking together in the Faubourg St. Ger-
main, we saw the funeral of a person of rank. I
remarked on Theodore's face a change, which in-
creased as the procession defiled past us. The
moment he perceived the coffin he started again,

and threw himself on my breast. "What is the matter with you?" said I. "It makes me remember," said he by signs, "that a short time before I was brought to Paris, I followed also in a black cloak the coffin of that magistrate who had caressed me so much: everybody was weeping, and I wept also." I augured from this second sign that he was an orphan, the heir of a large fortune which, doubtless, had tempted avaricious relatives to take advantage of the infirmity of the afflicted boy, to invade his rights, banish him, and ruin him for ever. These important discoveries redoubled my zeal and courage. Theodore became every day more interesting, and I conceived the project of re-instating him in his home.—But how to find it? The poor fellow had never heard the name of his father pronounced—he was ignorant of the spot where he was born, and of the family to which he belonged. I asked him if he well recollected the moment when he saw Paris for the first time. He assured me that it was incessantly present to his memory, and that he still saw the gate through which he had entered. The very next day beheld us visiting all the gates of Paris. Approaching that called Enfer, my pupil made me a sign that he recognized it; that it was here their carriage had been searched, that here he had alighted from it with two persons who accompanied him, and whose faces he perfectly well remembered. These fresh communications convinced me that he had arrived from the South; and upon his adding that he had passed several nights on the journey, and had changed horses from time to time, I calculated the time and distance, and no longer doubted that the native place of Theodore was one of the principal cities in the South of France.

FRANVAL. Oh! how great and penetrating is genius directed by the love of man! Go on! go on!

DE L'EPÉE. After writing a thousand useless missives to the cities of the South, I resolved to

visit them myself with Theodore, then too full of
memories not to recognize easily his native place.
The enterprize was long and painful : to be suc-
cessful, it was necessary to travel on foot. I am
old, but Heaven supported me. Notwithstanding
my age and infirmities, I left Paris sixty-six days
ago : alone with my pupil I quitted it by the
Enfer Gate, which he again recognized; and
there, after embracing each other, we invoked the
Eternal Father, and walked forth under His
auspices. We have gone through, successively,
several considerable cities. Theodore, carried
away by the desire of finding his home, often led
me to places he could not remember; my strength
was beginning to fail, and hope to abandon me
for ever, when this morning we arrived at the
gates of Toulouse.

FRANVAL (with vivacity). Well ?

*(Clemence rises, approaches De l' Epée, and leans on
the back of her mother's arm-chair.)*

DE L'EPÉE. On entering this city, Theodore
seized my hand, making signs that he recognized
it. At every step as we advance his face grows
animated—his eyes fill with tears. We cross the
public walks. Suddenly he kneels down, his
hands raised towards heaven—rises, and announces
to me that he has found his native place. Intoxi-
cated with joy, I forget like him the fatigue of the
journey : we traverse several parts, and on seeing
this large mansion which faces yours, Theodore
utters a cry, falls almost breathless into my arms,
and points to it as the house of his father. I make
enquiries, and am informed that it formerly belonged to the Counts of Harancour, of whom my
pupil is the only scion; that this mansion and all his
other possessions are in the hands of a Mr. Darlemont, his guardian and maternal uncle, who took
possession of it upon a certificate of his death, the
falsehood of which is proved by every circumstance.
I then enquire what Counsellor in this city can

direct me in this important affair,—you are pointed out to me as the most celebrated, and I come, Sir, to entrust to you all that I hold most dear, the fruit of eight years of labour, and the fate of my dear Theodore. God gave him to me to finish His work. I place him at this moment in your hands to restore to him what is most precious to man, a lawful and respectable name, and the in-alienable rights which nature and our laws bestow.

FRANVAL (with all the fire of enthusiasm and feeling rises, as also does his mother). Depend upon my care ; depend upon all the zeal which a man like you inspires ! Oh ! if ever I was happy and proud of my profession, it is at this moment ! But you can never imagine the delight I feel in being able to serve you ! (He wishes to kiss the hands of De l'Epée, who extends his arms and he immediately throws himself into them.)

DE L'EPÉE (with much emotion pressing Franval's hand) I am quite sure of you,—I see your tears fall.

Mrs. FRANVAL (with dignity). Who would not be moved, Sir, by the recital you have just made ?

CLEMENCE (in the greatest agitation). You have touched our hearts.

FRANVAL. It pains me to find a guilty man in the father of my friend : and first I ask to be allowed to use towards Darlemont all means which prudence and delicacy may dictate ; that failing, I will unmask the forger without pity, and will make him restore, in the name of the law, all the wealth he possesses, and of which he will then be, in my eyes, only a vile usurper.

Mrs. F. How I long to see this Darlemont sent back to the obscurity from which he rose.

CLEMENCE. And I, much more, to see his son there!

FRANVAL (to De l'Epée). But where have you left your Theodore ?

DE l'EPÉE. At an inn, where doubtless he is impatiently waiting for me.

FRANVAL. Ah! Why did you not bring him with you ?

31

CLEMENCE. How pleased I shall be to see him!

DE l'EPÉE. A Deaf-mute bears about always a something painful;——and I feared that his presence,—

FRANVAL. Might diminish the interest he inspires?

DE l'EPÉE (pressing Franval's hand). One is not sure always of meeting with hearts like yours.

FRANVAL. You must bring him to us. I wish to see him and know him. I dare even to ask more: the young man could not remain alone; and you and I will have to take many steps together without him; occupy rooms in my house, never shall I have more valued the charms of hospitality.

DE L'EPÉE. You are too kind; I should fear—

Mrs. FRANVAL (still with dignity). Sir, you will honour us and give us pleasure.

CLEMENCE (in the most persuasive tone). After such a long journey you must stand in need of repose; you will find nowhere the care that—that we will take of you.

DE L'EPÉE. I confess that I have not courage to resist such persuasives. I will return for my pupil immediately and introduce him to you.

FRANVAL. I, meantime, will think of our preliminary operations. I cannot conceal from you that they will be difficult. To have authentic records annulled, to tear a large fortune from the hands of an ambitious and powerful usurper, to convict him of forgery;—all this demands the greatest precaution.

DE L'EPÉE. I rely entirely on your talents and on your prudence. Whatever may be the result of this great undertaking, to have done my duty will be my consolation: and to have known you, Sir, (pressing Franval's hands) will be my reward.

(Exit; Franval, his Mother and Clemence conducting him, and returning into the room.)

END OF ACT II.

ACT III.

SCENE.—*The same as in Act II.*

CLEMENCE.—DOMINIC.

DOMINIC. No, Miss; no. Mr. St. Alme is not at home.

CLEMENCE. How unfortunate. His presence was never more wanted here.

DOMINIC (smiling significantly). He will come; be sure he'll come. If he had known with what impatience he would have been waited for, he would have taken good care not to absent himself thus. He is too anxious for opportunities of being with you to,—

CLEMENCE (quickly). Tell me, Dominic, have you executed my commission with Marianne?

DOMINIC. I should not forgive myself if I had forgotten it.

CLEMENCE. She accepted it without doubt.

DOMINIC. When I entered she was at her spinning-wheel. "Good morning, good mother."—"Your servant, Mr. Dominic. How is my beauty, my angel?" for she always calls you so. "Quite well, Marianne: And you?" "Oh! me? So-so, my rheumatism still troubles me; nevertheless I must work to support this poor life." "Here," said I, "there's something to help you."—"What! Two sovereigns!" "From Miss Clemence." "Just like her," cried she, and began directly to kiss repeatedly the gold pieces, and to pray Heaven to bless and keep you. And I don't think the day will pass without her coming to show her gratitude.

CLEMENCE. Good Marianne! How sweet it is to be able to give her some help. I shall never forget the care she lavished upon me during my illness. If she come, Dominic, you will take care that she speaks to me alone; do you understand?

DOMINIC. Be easy: the poor dear woman! how

different when her husband was porter at the Harancour House. They wanted nothing then; but Mr. Darlemont turned them away without pity, as well as all the others who had served the deceased President, his brother-in-law. The unhappy porter died of grief, and I know several of his old companions who, if it had not been for the help of Mr. St. Alme,—

CLEMENCE. It is certain that this gentleman seems to have made it his duty to repair the wrongs done by his father.

DOMINIC. Just as much as the one is harsh, haughty, and reserved, so much is the other easy, unaffected, and generous. Oh! he will be a good master, this latter,—an excellent head of a family (looking at Clemence with a smile), and especially a good husband. Don't you think so, Miss?

CLEMENCE (embarrassed). Yes,—I think that she—who may be able to decide the choice of this young man,—

DOMINIC (mysteriously and merrily). It is already done.

CLEMENCE. Indeed?

DOMINIC. I am sure of it.

CLEMENCE. Really: I have heard that he is to marry the daughter of the President.

DOMINIC. I have heard so, too—but that marriage will never come to pass.

CLEMENCE. Do you think so?

DOMINIC. We love some one else.

CLEMENCE. Ha! ha!

DOMINIC. Yes: we prefer happiness to riches: every one to his taste,—and, as to that, we have chosen in secret a charming lady,—

CLEMENCE (briskly). Have you prepared the rooms intended for the two strangers?

DOMINIC. No, not yet.

CLEMENCE. But go, then, Dominic. They will be here directly.

DOMINIC. Well, I'll go, I'll go. (Aside, as he

goes away) I shall never be able to make her confess that she is in love,—no, I shall never be able to make her acknowledge it. (Exit tittering.)

CLEMENCE (alone). That old servant delights in tormenting me. I felt myself blush at every word, and began to feel a confusion which it would have been impossible for me to conceal much longer.— But I will think only of the important discovery of this venerable De l'Epée, and will give myself up to all the hope it brings me. If Mr. Darlemont restore the wealth he possesses, there would no longer exist any distance between me and his son; and love, which ambitious pride would enchain, love would resume its empire.—But dare I hope that my insulted mother,—here she comes.

(Enter Franval, in black coat, with long hair, and Mrs. F.)

Mrs. F. Why, then, do you hesitate to give up this usurper to the vengeance of the law?—To shield crime, my son, is to become an accomplice.

FRANVAL. Can I forget that Darlemont is the father of my friend? (To Clemence) Has Dominic been to tell St. Alme to come here?

CLEMENCE. Yes, brother; but your friend had not yet returned.

Mrs. F. (seats herself). I cannot conceal from you, son, that after the letter I recently received, it is quite repugnant to my feelings to receive that young man here.

FRANVAL. Ought we to make him suffer for the faults of his father?

CLEMENCE. Far from sharing them, I assure you, dear mother, that he thinks only of how to remedy them, and make them forgotten.

Mrs. F. (with vehemence). As for me, I shall never forget the letter he had the audacity to write to me.

FRANVAL. If it were a question as to the guilty Darlemont only, I would unsparingly rend the veil with which the impostor covers himself; but such is the abuse of the prejudices which enslave

35

us, that I cannot unmask this forger without making the disgrace he merits recoil on his innocent son.

CLEMENCE (with increasing warmth). Oh! yes, entirely innocent. How many times, in our presence, has he lamented the loss of his cousin! What tears, truly touching, has he not shed before us, over the memory of the companion of his childhood. More frankness and delicacy cannot be united,—there cannot be a more generous and sensitive heart—(a severe look from Mrs. F. stops her, and makes her change her tone). Is it not true, brother?

FRANVAL (embarrassed, looking fixedly at his mother). One need see St. Alme only for one instant to remark in him—(enter Theodore and De l'Epée).—But here are our two guests.

Mrs. F. (rises).

DE L'EPÉE. Here is my Theodore, my adopted child, whom I have the honour of presenting to you.

THEODORE (bows to all. After having looked at Mr. and Mrs. Franval, he fixes his eyes upon Clemence).

CLEMENCE. What an interesting face!

Mrs. FRANVAL (approaching and examining him). He is the living likeness of his deceased father.

DE L'EPÉE (in a significant tone). Do you think so, Madam?

Mrs. F. On my honour I think I see President Harancour again.

THEODORE (turns his eyes upon Franval, whom he looks at a long time, seeming to study him).

FRANVAL. One can read in his face the impression of feeling, and an indescribably imposing air which announces the happy effects of the genius of his master.

THEODORE (after having looked fixedly at Franval, makes several signs to De l'Epée—laying his right hand on his forehead, holding it there a moment with the expression of genius—then stretching the right arm forward with force and dignity).

FRANVAL. What does he mean by those signs?

DE L'EPÉE. He tells me, Sir, that he reads on your face the certainty of triumphing in his cause, and of confounding his oppressor.

FRANVAL (with energy). Yes, I promise—and I will fulfil it. (They shake hands.)

THEODORE (after having with sadness laid his hand on his mouth and both his ears, takes one of Franval's hands, places it with one hand upon his heart, and with the other strikes briskly several times upon that of Franval).

FRANVAL. What is he saying to you now?

DE L'EPÉE (explaining every sign of Theodore). "That he cannot express his gratitude to you, but that you can feel by the beating of his heart, that your name is already engraved there for ever." They are his own expressions.

FRANVAL (with surprise and emotion). His own expressions! What! You understand each other so far as to comprehend all that he wishes to express?

DE L'EPÉE. Absolutely all.

Mrs. F. And he understands you as well?

THEODORE (rests his eyes again upon Clemence).

DE L'EPÉE. Without doubt. It is by these means that I have been able to adorn his mind and form his heart.

CLEMENCE. It is singular how his eyes are fixed upon me.

DE L'EPÉE. Do not be surprised, young lady; everything that presents to him the image of the truly beautiful, strikes him and fixes his thoughts. Nature, to recompense these unfortunate children for the wrongs she has done them, has given them delicacy of instinct, and rapidity of imagination,—therefore their intelligence, once developed, goes much further than ours. I reckon amongst my pupils profound mathematicians, historians, and distinguished men of letters. He, whom you see here, gained last winter a prize for poetry, and was crowned in a renowned lyceum, to the great astonishment of his competitors.

FRANVAL. I recollect, indeed, that the public papers announced this phenomenon, and consigned your name to immortality.

CLEMENCE. What! Can it be possible that this interesting young man, although deprived of speech and hearing, understands everything, expresses everything?

DE L'EPÉE. And answers immediately any questions you may wish to put to him. I will give you a proof:—

(He makes several signs to Theodore, touching first his shoulder to command his attention, carries the straightened fingers of his right hand to his forehead, and leaves them there an instant, then points with the forefinger to Clemence, and pretends to write several lines on his left hand.)

THEODORE, after showing that he understands the signs of De l'Epée, goes and seats himself at Franval's bureau, takes a pen, and prepares to write.

DE L'EPÉE (to Clemence). Put any question you choose to him—he will write it on seeing my signs, and will immediately add his answer. He is waiting for you.

CLEMENCE (with timidity). I don't know what question to ask.

DE L'EPÉE. The first that comes into your head.

CLEMENCE. Who is, in your opinion, the greatest living man in France?

DE L'EPÉE (after having considered an instant). It is a delicate question. Be so good as to ask it again, and pronounce slowly, as if you were dictating to him yourself.

THEODORE expresses by pantomime that he understands the signs De l'Epée makes, and writes every time he stops.

CLEMENCE. Who is, (De l'Epée signs to Theodore by throwing both hands forward, the fingers straight and the nails towards the floor; then with the forefinger of the right hand he describes a half-circle from the right to the left)—in your opinion—(De l'Epée raises the fingers of his right hand to his forehead and keeps them there an instant, then points to Theodore with his right fore-finger)—the greatest living man—(De l'Epée raises his right hand three times, then both hands as high as possible, brings them down on each shoulder, over the breast to his waist: he expresses "living" by breathing once with great force and touching the pulse at each wrist)—in France? (De l'Epée raises both hands above his head, and points all around.*)

DE L'EPÉE (taking the paper on which Theodore has written, and presenting it to Clemence). You see, first, that he has written the question with precision.

FRANVAL (examining the paper). And, above all, with one correction!

DE L'EPÉE gives back the paper to Theodore, who is motionless and thoughtful.

CLEMENCE. He looks puzzled.

DE L'EPÉE. One would be puzzled, at least, Miss Franval. The choice which you desire is difficult to make.

THEODORE rouses from his reverie, grows animated by degrees, and writes.

FRANVAL (watching all Theodore's movements). What fire in his looks! What vivacity in all his motions! He seems at once touched and satisfied. I shall be much deceived if his answer do not bear the impression of a sensitive heart and an enlightened mind.

THEODORE rises and gives the paper to Clemence, making her a sign to read it. Franval and his

These signs must be very distinct, but quick, and so as not to interrupt the scene.

mother approach eagerly. Theodore stands near De l'Epée, whom he looks at enquiringly.

CLEMENCE (reading) Question.—Who is, in your opinion, the greatest living man in France?

Answer.—Nature names Buffon; science indicates Dalembert; feeling and truth claim Jean Jacques Rousseau; wit and taste point to Voltaire; but genius and humanity proclaim De l'Epée. I prefer him to all the others.

(THEODORE makes several signs, expressing a balance by raising and lowering each hand in turn; then raising his right hand as high as possible and pointing to De l'Epée with the fore-finger, then falls upon De l'Epée's breast and presses him in his arms.)

DE L'EPÉE (with emotion, which he endeavours to repress). You must pardon him this mistake— it is the enthusiasm of gratitude. (He embraces Theodore again.)

FRANVAL (taking the paper from Clemence and examining it again). I cannot recover from my astonishment.

Mrs. F. One must see such a miracle to believe it.

CLEMENCE. One cannot help being moved, even to tears.

FRANVAL. This answer proves a purity of taste, announces an extent of knowledge! (To De l'Epée) What research, calculation, and care, you must have bestowed, in order to achieve these great results!

DE L'EPÉE. To say what it has cost me, is impossible; but the idea of restoring a mind! (pointing to Theodore) this sublime idea gives strength and courage! If the labouring man, on seeing the rich harvest which covers the fields he has tilled, experience a joy in proportion to his labour, judge what I must feel, when in the midst of my pupils, I see these afflicted children pierce by little and little the gloom which surrounds them; awake at the first dawn of superior intelligence; and attain by degrees the inexpressible happiness of communicating their ideas : thus I form around me an interesting family, of whom I am the happy father. There are more dazzling pleasures, there are pleasures more easily enjoyed; but I doubt whether all nature furnishes a truer pleasure.

FRANVAL. Believe also that of all the great men whom your interesting Theodore has just classified with so much justice, there is not one whose name will survive for posterity longer than your own. If France raise statues to heroes who by their exploits contributed to her glory, can she refuse one to him who, by his creative genius, by his unwearying labour and inimitable patience has become the repairer of Nature's defects !

(Enter Dominic and Marianne.)

DOMINIC (to Marianne still behind the scenes). But I tell you, good Marianne, you cannot speak to her.

MARIANNE (entering and standing still in the middle of the stage between Franval and Mrs. F.) Prevent my seeing her and pressing her to my bosom, you'll never manage it, Mr. Dominic.

DOMINIC (aside to Clemence). It was impossible for me to hinder her coming in.

THEODORE (looks at Marianne, and appears struck with some remembrance).

MARIANNE (with volubility and feeling, to Mrs. F.) Excuse me, Madam, if I take the liberty—(to Franval) Sir, I am sorry to interrupt you, but when my heart is full I must absolutely,—good, dear Miss Clemence! condescending continually to think of me, providing for all my wants, and sending me—

CLEMENCE (interrupting her). It is nothing, dear Marianne, it is not worth—

MARIANNE. Not worth ?—

Mrs. F. Tell me, my dear, what all this means ?

THEODORE watches every movement of Marianne with the greatest emotion, and makes signs to De l'Epée of some one ringing a door bell, and of a

woman opening the door, and points to Marianne.
De l'Epée follows these signs with demonstrations
of astonishment and joy.

MARIANNE. Her modesty forbids her answering,
but I will tell you all about it. You must know
then, Madam, that since the illness of this dear
child, she is always sending me clothes and pro-
visions; at last, this very morning, two sovereigns
by Mr. Dominic. It gave me the power in my
turn, of helping a poor neighbour—(seizing and
kissing Clemence's hand)—how sweet it is for
Marianne to owe you all that!

DEL'EPÉE (running to Marianne). Good woman,
good woman.

MARIANNE (with respect and astonishment). Sir!

DE L'EPÉE. Did you not live some long time
with the family of Harancour.

MARIANNE. My dead husband was porter there
five and thirty years.

DE L'EPÉE. Do you remember having seen
little Julius there, who was born deaf and dumb?

MARIANNE. Do I remember him?—His death
cost us too dear for me ever to forget him.

DE L'EPÉE (leading Marianne opposite Theodore,
who looks at her intently). Well, look, look at
this young man!

MARIANNE (staring closely at Theodore). What
do I see? Hey! But—

THEODORE, having brushed back the hair which
covers his face, turns it towards Marianne, and
makes a sign to her that she carried him in her
arms when he was a child.

MARIANNE. 'Tis he!—he whom we loved so
much! whom we so lamented! Yes, oh! yes, I
recognise him! (She falls at Theodore's feet; he
raises her immediately, and presses her in his arms.)

DOMINIC. And I who was so obstinate, pre-
venting her coming in!

DE L'EPÉE. Singular and precious discovery!

FRANVAL. Which will lead us, it cannot be
doubted, to important proofs.

Mrs. F.   And confound that insolent Darlemont!
I am in such joy.

CLEMENCE.   My joy is still greater—I privately
assist an unfortunate woman—and thus I procure
the first witness—O heavenly kindness!

MARIANNE.   Ah! if my poor husband were alive
now!   But how can it be that this dear child, who
was said to be dead, is come back to this city? By
what providence, which I cannot comprehend.

DE L'EPÉE.   You shall know all good mother.
But tell me, are you sufficiently convinced that
this is Julius Harancour, to attest it in a court of
justice.

MARIANNE. I will maintain it before God and man.

FRANVAL.   Could you not procure us the testimony of some old servants who, like yourself,
have known the young Count in his childhood?

MARIANNE.   Certainly. The coachman's widow
is still alive.

DOMINIC.   Peter, the old groom, came to see me
the other day with his wife: they don't live far
from here.

MRS. FRANVAL (quickly). You must go and fetch
them all, immediately.

DOMINIC.   I will run.

FRANVAL (stopping Dominic).   One moment;—
(to De l'Epée) I have already told you that the
friendship which unites me to St. Alme, imposes
upon me the duty of acting with discretion: I
propose, therefore, that we should first go to
Harancour House.   There we will attack Darlemont—you with an irresistible weapon, as the interpreter of Nature, I with the language of the law,
with all the force which so noble a cause inspires;
and this man, how audacious soever he may be,
will be very bold if he repel our efforts.

DE L'EPÉE.   I adopt your plan, and I think of
a means which may probably insure our success.
(He retires with Theodore, to whom he explains
by signs the resolution which they have just formed.)

FRANVAL. I desire you all to keep profound silence as to what has just taken place.

MARIANNE. I promise.

DOMINIC. Be easy.

(They all three rejoin De l' Epée and Theodore.)

Mrs. F. As for me, I promise nothing.

CLEMENCE (giving her her arm). But, dear mother,—

Mrs. F. (with bitterness as they walk away). Yes, my dear, you may say what you like, I do not know how to prevent myself crying out aloud against this Darlemont—this ambitious wretch who must be punished, this insolent fellow who must be humbled.

(They rejoin the other personages, and the curtain falls.)

END OF ACT III.

ACT IV.

A drawing-room in Harancour House, richly and sumptuously furnished—on the left hand is a door leading to Darlemont's room.

(By the side door enter Dubois, Darlemont, and lastly Dupré, who appears gloomy and pre-occupied.)

DARLEMONT. You say my son is not yet come back?

DUBOIS. No, Sir.

DARLEMONT. And that he forbade you to follow him ?

DUBOIS. Yes, Sir.

DARLEMONT. Can he have returned to Franval's house ?

DUBOIS. It does not appear so—for the Counsellor has just sent again to enquire for him.

DARLEMONT (to Dubois). Go and wait for him in the porter's lodge : as soon as he enters you will tell him to come to me immediately. Do you hear ?—immediately. *(Exit Dubois.)*

DARLEMONT. Well, Dupré, what do you want with me?

DUPRÉ (taking a purse out of his pocket, and laying it on a table). I am come, Sir, to return you the twenty-five sovereigns which you sent me this morning

DARLEMONT. Return them! And why? It is the amount of the first six months of the annuity I insured for you the other day, in reward for your services. I desire that every term should be punctually paid to you in advance.

DUPRÉ. Take back this gold, I say. It is impossible for me to receive a reward for an action which will always weigh heavy on my heart.

DARLEMONT. Will you never forget, then, that boy, Harancour.

DUPRÉ. He is incessantly in my thoughts. I can still see the last look he cast upon me when you separated us.

DARLEMONT (bluntly). I could not bear the sight of that Mute—that wearisome automaton!

DUPRÉ. However, you will agree with me that everything in him showed a good disposition, an excellent heart. As quite a little fellow, when he took a walk with me, he never met a poor creature without making a sign for me to give something; he had no greater pleasure than sharing with others all he possessed. And that day when he saved the life of your son, whose giddiness and vivacity—Mr. St. Alme was throwing stones at a great farm-yard dog, and it jumped upon him and threw him down. Julius, frightened at the danger which threatened his cousin, rushed, quick as lightning, on the furious animal, and received on his right arm a severe wound, the scar of which will last his life long.

DARLEMONT. You are always telling me of that adventure.

DUPRÉ. Because it proves that the young Count

had as much courage as goodness ; and who knew better than I that touching goodness ? I, his father's old valet ; I, to whom he had been entrusted from his infancy ! and yet I could abandon him ; I could yield to your persuasions and become your accomplice !

DARLEMONT (with passion). Dupré !

DUPRÉ (with heat). Yes, Sir, your accomplice ! when one has destroyed the peace of mind of an old servant, one ought to listen to his complaints, and respect his grief.

DARLEMONT (restraining a passionate movement). My dear Dupré, the excess of your sensibility quite misleads you. Would you, then, after eight whole years reveal the important secret I confided to you ?

DUPRÉ. What good would that do me ? where could we find, now, the unfortunate child ? I promised secrecy upon all that has passed between us ; and I will keep my word on condition, Sir, that you will never speak to me of that fatal pension, which you thought would seduce me. I have quite enough remorse, without aggravating it by disgraceful wages.—(Darlemont is impatient.) Yes, Sir, disgraceful.

(Exit Dupré by the side door.)

DARLEMONT (alone). I am anxious and tormented by the grief of that old man. How hard it is to have to depend on a witness of our secret actions ! But what have I to fear ? Transported suddenly a hundred and sixty miles from his home, skilfully lost in the middle of Paris, Julius, without doubt, was taken to some house of public charity ; perhaps, even he is dead by this time—in any case, what intelligence could be given by a Deaf-Mute, an orphan, and claimed by no one ? However, if Dupré should happen to divulge—I cannot be too careful of that old man ; I must absolutely accommodate myself to him, overcome my pride, my temper, and above all things not lose sight of him an instant. O fortune! fortune! what humiliations must I submit to for you, and how dear does it cost me to insure my enjoyment of you.

(Enter St. Alme by the side door.)

ST. ALME. I am told you are enquiring for me, father.

DARLEMONT. Yes, I wish to have another conversation with you; I warn you that it will be the last if you do not yield for ever to the will of your father. But tell me, St. Alme, what has become of you all the morning?

ST. ALME (with openness). Father,—for I cannot dissemble—I tell you frankly that I am just come from the house of President Argental.

DARLEMONT (with dismay). And what did you go there for, without me?

ST. ALME. To open my heart fully to him—to inform him myself of my love for Miss Franval.

DARLEMONT (vehemently). You have had that temerity?—(with concentrated rage)—and what answer did you receive from the President?

ST. ALME (with confidence and joy). O father! what a noble and generous soul!—ah! I was right in what I thought of him.

DARLEMONT (still restraining his anger with an effort). What did he say to you? Answer!

ST. ALME. These are his own words. "It would have been sweet to my heart—the consolation of my old age to have united you to my daughter, but the choice you have made in Miss Franval is unexceptionable."

DARLEMONT. What?

ST. ALME. "The ties which attach you to so perfect a being must be indissoluble."

DARLEMONT (with a shout). Indissoluble!

ST. ALME. I see that this recital makes you angry.

DARLEMONT. Go on; finish.

ST. ALME (hesitating, and in the greatest uneasiness). In fact, he assured me that far from being hurt by my proceeding, he honoured my intentions and appreciated my frankness. (A convulsive movement from Darlemont.) He promised to exert all his influence over you to make you consent—(another movement from Darlemont)—and I do not doubt he will soon be here himself to intercede for me.

DARLEMONT. And could you believe that I would yield to his solicitations; that I would be the plaything of your audacity ?

ST. ALME. Father!

DARLEMONT. Never was mortal man more unhappy than I! I become the possessor, (hesitating), of a considerable inheritance. I wish to employ it by gaining for my only son an alliance envied by the first families in the country; and when I have at length overcome all obstacles—conquered by dint of money, all prejudices and distances—I find only an ungrateful son who trifles with my kindness, who disdains at once an immense fortune and the highest rank in the magistracy. Mad man, thus to reject opulence, you do not know what it costs to gain it—(seizing him by the arm, and leading him forward). No, you do not know what it costs!

ST. ALME. Father, whatever may have been the sacrifices your fortune has cost you, they cannot be compared to those you require from me ;— I not only love,—adore,—but I can now confide to you that I am beloved in return.

DARLEMONT. Who has assured you of this ?

ST. ALME. Clemence herself—

DARLEMONT. Can you prefer to the advantages I propose the interested avowal of a fortuneless girl, the cunning, seductive plots—

ST. ALME. Father! You may rend this too confiding, too sensitive heart; you may try everything to uproot my love; but spare me the pain of hearing her I love insulted.—Such an effort is beyond my power.—Yes, Clemence has won me for ever, but it was without artifice or design—her attractions, her virtue, the respectable family whence she springs, these are the sole plots, the sole cunning of this adorable girl—these are the only seductions she has employed to gain your son.

DARLEMONT (with an embarrassed, confused movement). For the last time listen to the command of your father. You must give up Miss Franval.

ST. ALME. Rather, a hundred times, death!

DARLEMONT (gently). My peace depends upon it.

ST. ALME. My life depends upon it.

DARLEMONT (still more gently). Yield to my wishes.

ST. ALME. I am beloved!

DARLEMONT. St. Alme, I conjure you: (pressing him in his arms.)

ST. ALME (in the most tender tone and kissing Darlemont's hands). I am beloved, father—I am beloved!

DARLEMONT (repulsing him with fury). It is enough—go.

ST. ALME. (Again kissing his hand.) Go!

(Then after pantomimic signs between him and Darlemont, he goes out by the side door.)

DARLEMONT (alone, after a moment of silence and stupor). I shall never be able to overcome this violent love, this devouring attachment. His union with the only daughter of President Argental would have made my rank equal with my riches, would have sheltered me for ever from all anxiety. My dearest hope, my only ambition, everything has vanished!

(Dubois enters by the door at the back.)

DUBOIS. Sir, Counsellor Franval requests a private conversation with you.

DARLEMONT. Counsellor Franval!

DUBOIS. Yes, Sir.

DARLEMONT (after reflecting a moment). Tell him I cannot be seen.

(Exit Dubois.)

DARLEMONT (alone). He comes to win me to his side; to tell about his sister and the marriage he projects with my son; it is a concerted plot between them, which I know how to upset for ever. These lawyers with their great reputation imagine they can rival rank and fortune. I am very glad to humble the pride of this one and let him know—.

DUBOIS (entering). Mr. Franval sends me back to announce to you that he is accompanied by L'Abbé De l'Epée?

DARLEMONT. L'Abbé De l'Epée!

DUBOIS. Instructor of the Deaf-mutes at Paris.

DARLEMONT (thunder-stricken). L'Abbé De l'Epée—

DUBOIS. And that they have to communicate to you, Sir, most important matters.

DARLEMONT (aside in the greatest trouble). What presentiments!—it seems as if everything combined—one would say, that fate takes pleasure in tormenting me.

DUBOIS. What are your orders, Sir?

DARLEMONT (appearing to arm himself with resolution). Well, let them come in.
(Exit Dubois.)

DARLEMONT (alone, walking about in the greatest agitation). My doubts are too cruel; I must clear them up. What can bring this celebrated man here? Why does he address himself to me; why wish for an interview? I shall never have a moment's peace!—They are coming; let me compose myself, and try by a firm, imposing attitude to dispel even the least suspicion.

(DUBOIS introduces De l'Epée and Franval, and after placing seats he goes out, on a sign from Darlemont.)

DE L'EPÉE (to Darlemont). Sir, I greet you.

DARLEMONT (after returning the salutation of both, and making them take seats). I am told you desire to speak to me in private.—May I ask from what motive?—

FRANVAL (with calm dignity). The interest which I take in the father of St. Alme, and the obligation of fulfilling a great act of justice, bring us here,

D

DARLEMONT. Explain yourself.

DE L'EPÉE (studying him). I am about to cause you a great surprise—know, then, that chance, or rather He who directs everything according to His will, has placed in my hands Count Julius Harancour, your nephew.

(DARLEMONT makes a terrified gesture.)

FRANVAL. Yes, that young Deaf-mute, whose guardian you were, who is still alive, and who claims, by the voice of Mr. De l'Epée, his fortune and his name.

DARLEMONT (trying to conceal his confusion). Julius, do you say,—still lives?

DE L'EPÉE. God has recompensed me by sparing his life.

DARLEMONT. I should rejoice at it,—but it is a tale I cannot believe—the young Count died at Paris, nearly eight years ago.

DE L'EPÉE (looking fixedly at him). Are you quite sure of it?

FRANVAL. You may have been mistaken.

DARLEMONT. I was, myself, with him, and—

DE L'EPÉE (still looking at him, and close to him). You were present at his last moments?— You saw the remains, as we say, of this unfortunate child?

DARLEMONT (embarrassed). Without entering into all these questions, it will suffice if I tell you that the death of Julius Harancour was, at the time, proved by a legal and authentic act.

DE L'EPÉE (with his eyes still fixed on Darlemont). The falsehood of which has been proved to me, and at this moment more plainly than ever.

DARLEMONT (with greater embarrassment). And upon what can you found such a conviction?

DE L'EPÉE. Pardon my frankness,—but this confusion, this embarrassment,—everything betrays you in spite of yourself.

DARLEMONT (rising). Could you dare to suspect me?——

De l'Epée (rising also). He who during sixty years has studied nature, deciphered every movement, every emotion, easily reads the heart of man. I needed but a single glance to unravel what is passing in yours.

Darlemont. My conscience does not reproach me. I owe you no explanation—What entitles you both,—with what right, in fact, do you both come here?—

De l'Epée. What right have I?—The right which eight years of toil, care, and patience give : the right which every compassionate man has of helping his fellow creatures.—What authorizes me? —'Tis this: God entrusted Julius Harancour to me, to cherish, to instruct, to avenge ; and I obey His eternal decree.

Darlemont. To avenge Julius Harancour ?—

Franval. My rights also are not less sacred. First, I have the confidence of this celebrated man, who has made choice of me to finish his work, the noblest which ever did honour to humanity. Secondly, my profession imposes upon me the duty of defending the weak against the powerful, of extending my hand to protect the oppressed.

Darlemont. Of what oppression do you accuse me ?

Franval. What authorizes me is the sole desire of adjusting matters between you and the young Count.

Darlemont. I do not understand you.

Franval. Nothing can save you from his claims :—guilty or not, you can still retrieve all :— confide in my zeal, and believe that after the interests of the orphan, whose defender I am,— there is nothing,—no, nothing, which is dearer to me in the world than the honour of the father of my friend.

Darlemont. But, once more, upon what proofs, upon what indications can you imagine that this Deaf-mute, for whom you interest yourselves so strongly, can be the heir of the Earls of Harancour?

FRANVAL. Everything combines to prove his identity.

DE L'EPÉE. The agreement of the time when he was brought to me, with that when you conducted him to Paris,—

FRANVAL. With that when the report of his death was circulated here,—his age,—his affliction ;—

DE L'EPÉE. A striking resemblance to his father.

DARLEMONT. A resemblance !

DE L'EPÉE. His joy, his emotion on entering this city, on recognizing this mansion ;—

FRANVAL. The discovery he has already made of an old servant of his father's ;—

DE L'EPÉE. In fine, the avowals of your ward himself,—

DARLEMONT (struck by every detail). Avowals !

FRANVAL. The information which he gives with confidence, with precision ;—

DARLEMONT. Information !

DE L'EPÉE. That astonishes you !—you were far from suspecting that an unfortunate Deaf-mute,—

FRANVAL. Know, then, that Julius has found in Mr. De l'Epée a second father ; that guided by his lessons, instructed by his virtues, influenced by his genius, he is, at the present time, the most perfect model of an educated man. Well informed on the past, full of experience as to the present, nothing escapes his penetration, everything is impressed on his memory.—Yourself,—

DARLEMONT (quickly, and with confusion which increases till the end of the scene). No, no ; never will I recognize in this unknown youth, him,— whose death was but too certain,—and I will, before the tribunal,—

FRANVAL. Beware of appearing there ; reflect that there is more than one amongst the elder judges who would recognize, in this orphan, the features of a magistrate whose memory is still honoured in Toulouse; reflect that there is not a single inhabitant of this city who would not be moved by the sight of the young Count, by the recital of what this friend of humanity has done for him, by the appearance of that venerable head, the white hairs of which are an image of his numberless benefactions—beware, I repeat, of the tribunal;—you would be condemned, you would be dishonoured for ever.

DARLEMONT. I am proof against fear — and though even the certificate of the death of Julius Harancour should be delared false, the law could touch only those who signed it.

FRANVAL. And if those witnesses accuse you of having bribed them, and of being their accomplice, you will not be able to escape the vengeance of the law, but will share their punishment and infamy.—You tremble?—

DE L'EPÉE. Your mouth is ready to reveal the secret of your heart; do not restrain it.

FRANVAL. Give utterance to the torments which so long have brooded in your breast.

DE L'EPÉE. You have no idea how the weight of a crime is lightened by the confession of it.

FRANVAL (taking one of his hands). Yield to our advice—

DE L'EPÉE (taking his other hand). Yield to our entreaties.

DARLEMONT (with force, and tearing himself suddenly from them). Leave me.—Leave me. (He advances and stands a moment with his face in his hands.)

DE L'EPÉE (aside to Franval). His mind is wavering. Let us bring him the last proof. (He runs to the door where he makes a sign. Theodore appears immediately, conducted by Marianne, who stands aside. De l'Epée hurriedly brings Theodore near Darlemont, and places him so that he shall be the first object which strikes the sight of the latter when he turns his head. De l'Epée and Franval watch all his movements.)

DARLEMONT (aside). These two men have an influence,—a penetration,—I must resist them. (He resumes an imposing attitude, turns his head and perceives Theodore)—My God !—

(He stands motionless, as if thunder-struck.)

THEODORE, after having looked fixedly at Darlemont, utters a cry of horror and runs for protection to De l'Epée, to whom he makes a sign that he recognizes his guardian, pointing to Darlemont.

DE L'EPÉE. Do you doubt now that Julius Harancour is still alive ?

DARLEMONT. He !—My nephew !

FRANVAL. What ! Can you still maintain—

DARLEMONT. If he were Julius—would he flee from me thus—would he not rather have thrown himself into my arms ?

DE L'EPÉE. If he were not Julius would he, on seeing you, have shown that terror which a pure mind feels at the first sight of the author of his misfortunes ? ' Oh ! If I had doubted till this moment that he was your ward, this single touch of nature would have been sufficient to convince me.

DARLEMONT (without looking at Theodore or De l'Epée). I disown him, I tell you, and I will always disown him, till by judicial proofs——

DE L'EPÉE (approaching Darlemont). You disown him, do you say ? How comes it, then, that your whole body trembles ?

DARLEMONT (with a new anxiety). Who ?—I ?—

DE L'EPÉE. Whence came that avenging cry which escaped you at the sight of the young Count ?

FRANVAL. Your eye cannot rest on the unfortunate youth—

DE L'EPÉE. You try in vain to struggle against nature, it has pronounced your sentence—

THEODORE at this time is making signs, with bent fingers down both sleeves of his coat, and down both legs, describing a child being stripped and then clothed with rags.

DE L'EPÉE (interprets these signs, saying), my

pupil himself assures me by his signs that he recognizes you; that it was you who conducted him to Paris, that it was you who,—

DARLEMONT (interrupting him roughly). Let us have no more!—I am tired of all this dunning—Get out of my house!

FRANVAL (with calmness and dignity). Your house!—We are in the house of Julius Harancour.

DARLEMONT (with passion, and in a very loud voice). Be gone, I say! or fear the effects of my anger. *(Enter St. Alme).*

ST. ALME. What a strange noise!—Can any one have dared to insult you, father?—Whom do I see?—Franval!

THEODORE during this speech recognizes St. Alme; he rushes towards him, uttering a cry of joy, pressing him in his arms and covers him with caresses.

ST. ALME. Who is this young man, whose caresses—

FRANVAL. It is Julius Harancour, your cousin—the ward of your father.—

ST. ALME (with extreme joy). Can it be true?

DARLEMONT (with energy and quickness). You are deceived, my son.

ST. ALME. No, no: although his features are changed by time, I feel that my heart—

DARLEMONT (to St. Alme with more energy). You are deceived, I tell you! It is a snare laid for us—

ST. ALME. A snare! And why?—

DARLEMONT. Yes, a snare!

ST. ALME. It is easy, however, to convince ourselves. (He raises the sleeve on Theodore's right arm, sees the scar, and exclaims)—'Tis he!

DARLEMONT. He?

ST. ALME. Yes, yes, there is the scar to which I owe my life. This is my deliverer. (They fall into each others arms.)

DARLEMONT. St. Alme, withdraw!

St. Alme (still holding Theodore in his arms). I! Repel Julius from my bosom?

Darlemont. Retire; or fear—

St. Alme. Though your malediction had fallen on me instantly, though a thunder-bolt had struck me before your eyes, I could not have helped starting at the sight of my first friend, the companion of my childhood.—I could not resist the voice of nature. (He presses Theodore again in his arms. Darlemont, in rage and confusion, turns and seats himself in an arm chair with his back towards the other persons.)

De l'Epée (to Darlemont, after a moment's silence). And can you be unmoved at this sight? Can you be insensible to the tears which I see in every eye?—Ah! Sir, how I pity you!

Franval (also to Darlemont). You must at last yield to the force of circumstances. It is no longer possible for you to resist; and, when your son himself—

St. Alme. Father, in the name of Heaven!—

Darlemont (vehemently, rising). Be silent! (To Franval and De l'Epée.) No, no; I do not acknowledge the Count in this Deaf-mute; and in spite of all that you may undertake, in spite of all the witnesses you may summon, I shall be able to maintain in full force the certificate of the death of Julius Harancour, and to support my rights. Rid me, therefore, of your presence, and quit my house, all of you.

De l'Epée (leading Theodore forward). Come, unfortunate but interesting orphan; reed, so long beaten by the storm. (Theodore here passes his finger across De l'Epée's eyes where he sees tears starting.) Come, if the law do not avenge thee, if imposture and cupidity drive thee from thy home, the heart and peaceful roof of old De l'Epée will still be thine.

St. Alme (with a motion of respect and surprise). De l'Epée!

(De l'Epée and Theodore, in retiring, cast a look upon Darlemont, who is still motionless, with downcast eyes. Marianne follows them, and they form a group.)

FRANVAL (to Darlemont). Though hitherto I have treated you with the respect which I owed to the father of St. Alme, (he presses with emotion the hand of St. Alme) you may rely now upon my 'using every means commanded by duty, and all the strength of my indignation—(he interrupts himself at a look from St. Alme). Whatever may be the obscurity in which you hope to conceal yourself, whatever your credit and your power, you shall not escape me ; no, you shall not escape me.

(He joins the group at the back, and they go off together.)

St. ALME (running, after Franval). Franval !— my friend, I will be with you in an instant.

DARLEMONT (rising, aside, whilst St. Alme is conducting Franval to the door). At last they are gone !

St. ALME (returning, after having shut the door). Father, pray listen to me.

DARLEMONT. Quit my presence also.

St. ALME. 'Tis Julius :—You cannot doubt it.

DARLEMONT. Leave me, unhappy boy.

St. ALME. You are ruining us, father.

DARLEMONT. 'Tis you, alone, undo us, senseless boy—your imprudence and indiscretion. But I shall be able to repair all. (He is going away, when St. Alme throwing himself on his knees holds him back by his coat.)

St. ALME. In the name of everything that is holy, yield not to the ambition which misleads you. Restore, restore the wealth which does not belong to you. (Darlemont makes a terrible effort to disengage himself from the hands of St. Alme, who is still holding by his clothes.) If you leave me without fortune I shall still have what is worth more, a name without reproach, and your memory

D 2

to cherish. (Darlemont drags him on his knees towards the side door). Father, you do not hear me, you fly from me, you turn away your eyes.— Father—(in heart-rending voice)—you dishonour us!—you dishonour us !

(He is dragged away by Darlemont, and the curtain falls.)

END OF ACT IV.

ACT V.

SCENE.—*The same as in Act II.*

THEODORE, FRANVAL, DE L'EPÉE, MRS. FRANVAL, CLEMENCE.

(Franval is writing at his desk ; Theodore seated near him intent over a book, occasionally moving the fingers of his right hand as is customary with Deaf-mutes when reading ; De l'Epée is walking up and down, by turns thinking, and talking to Franval about his writing. In the centre Mrs. Franval, seated in a large easy chair, is employed on some wool-work ; Clemence on her left, seated in a chair, with embroidery in her hand, but appears suffering and in anxiety, often looking at her brother.)

CLEMENCE. Dominic is gone a long time !

Mrs. F. He is so slow in everything he does !

FRANVAL (still writing). I feel,—in drawing up this deed of accusation,—an emotion I cannot restrain.

Mrs. F. I advise you, son, to try again, and not spare this Darlemont !

DE L'EPÉE (still walking). Imposture and audacity could not be carried further.—I could never have imagined he would have been able to resist our entreaties, and especially the sight of that unfortunate youth. (He points to Theodore, who is buried in his book.)

Mrs. F.   He is a usurper, and his punishment cannot come too soon.

FRANVAL.   I agree with you,—but his son!

CLEMENCE.   Who would not be interested in that young man?

(De l'Epée looks at Clemence as if he suspected her love for St. Alme.)

FRANVAL (ceasing to write).   At his very name alone, I feel my heart fail, and, in spite of myself, the pen falls from my hand.

DE L'EPÉE.   I perceive the full extent of your sacrifice, but my only hope is in you.

FRANVAL (forcibly).   You shall triumph; yes, your Theodore shall be avenged; (with feeling) but pardon this involuntary emotion, this just tribute to friendship.

DE L'EPÉE.   Could I blame these generous struggles!—Ah, believe, rather, that I share them.   If consideration could succeed, I would be the first to urge its being persisted in; but this ambitious Darlemont will yield only to force, will obey only the terrible voice of justice.

FRANVAL.   Yes, yes, terrible! This accusation once brought forward, nothing will save Darlemont from infamy, from the penalty pronounced by the law.   What will then become of his unhappy son, whose fiery soul and extreme sensibility—but I still flatter myself that he will prevent his father making any judicial exposure, the cruel consequence of which—

Mrs. F. (still working).   And I am quite sure he will not succeed in that.

CLEMENCE.   But, why? If a father's voice can restore a wandering child to virtue, that of a son,—and such a son as St. Alme, must have some power over a father's heart.

DE L'EPÉE (again looking at Clemence).   I think as Miss Clemence does.   I rely much, very much, on this young man.   (St. Alme enters, dejected, and stands without being perceived by anyone.)

FRANVAL (still writing). He is far from thinking that this hand, which has been so often pressed in his own, is, at this moment, tracing the accusation of his father. (St. Alme starts with terrible emotion, which he represses with difficulty.)

DE L'EPÉE(perceiving St. Alme). But here he is!

(A moment of general silence.)

ST. ALME (accosting Franval with reserve and dignity, Franval not venturing to look at him). You shall not hear a murmur.—What you have done, any other would have done.—There are circumstances when feeling must be silent and give place to duty. (Clemence lets her work fall, and appears in the greatest agitation.)

DE L'EPEE. Must I, to discharge the duty which Heaven entrusts to me, rend a heart like yours? You cannot imagine, Sir, how much I feel for you.

FRANVAL (to St. Alme). Think what is passing in my heart : on the one side the confidence I am honoured with (he points to De l'Epée), and the justice due to this oppressed young man (pointing to Theodore), command me to proceed ; on the other hand friendship binds me down. I can take no step without clashing against one or the other— do nothing without storing up regret for the future. Never were such torments endured at one time— never was man in so cruel a position !

ST. A. (pressing by turns the hands of De l'Epée and Franval). Ah! I was sure I should find in you this generous impulse, this painful difficulty.— (To De l'Epée,) I did not expect less than these touching words, this tender interest, so character- istic of the defender of the oppressed, the bene- factor of man. But as you have both fulfilled your duty, permit me, in my turn, to fulfil that which Nature prescribes, the defence of my father.

FRANVAL (quickly). Can you have obtained from Mr. Darlemont—

ST. A. (with sadness). He would not hear me ; he drove me from him. All that honour cherishes, that filial love holds most dear—nothing, nothing could bend him. He persists in desiring to prove the death of his ward; upon all the rest he maintains a ferocious silence. (He leans upon Franval.)

THEODORE perceives St. Alme in dejection, rises hastily, throws down his book, and goes to press his cousin in his arms.

FRANVAL. Dear St. Alme!

DE L'EPÉE (to St. Alme). Look at your young friend; one would think he had just heard you speak, and was trying to console you.

ST. A. (pressing Theodore to his heart). What joy I have in seeing him again! After such a long separation, must our happiness be blended with suffering and terror? But is it quite certain,— are you indeed both convinced that my father is guilty?

*(Enter Dupré, bareheaded and in the greatest
bewilderment).*

DUPRÉ (to Franval). Ah, Sir! Can it be true what Mr. Darlemont has just told me? Is the young Count Harancour—

FRANVAL (pointing to De l'Epée). Behold the man who saved him!

DUPRÉ. My God! (He sees Theodore, who is looking at him). Yes; 'tis he himself! At last I see him again!

THEODORE rushes towards Dupré, and wishes to embrace him.

DUPRÉ (drawing back and avoiding his caresses). He sees in me only the man who took care of him in infancy. He does not know that I am unworthy of his love, and that I, myself, contributed to his ruin.

ST. A. You, Dupré?

THEODORE, at several signs from De l'Epée, suspends all at once his caresses, remains motionless an instant, and draws back by degrees, fixing on Dupré a look full of surprise and grief.

DUPRÉ. But he must know all my remorse. He

must let me die at his feet. (He falls at the feet of Theodore.)

FRANVAL (raising him). Stand up, and tell us all.

ST. A. 'Twas he alone who accompanied my father when he conducted the young Count to Paris.

FRANVAL (to Duprè). It was about eight years ago ?

DUPRÉ. Yes, Sir.

ST. A. Well ?

DUPRÉ, The very evening of our arrival, Mr. Darlemont ordered me to procure some beggar's clothes, and put them on little Julius.

DE L'EPÉE. Exactly : it was in those rags that he was brought to me.

DUPRÉ. As soon as he was disguised, his uncle made him get into a cab with him, and they disappeared. Some hours after Mr. Darlemont returned alone. I shewed my surprise at this, and pressed him with questions. Then he confided to me that he had just executed a project he had long contemplated, and that he had lost the young Count in the midst of Paris.

ST. A. (suffocated and maddened). What! my father himself—could he have had the barbarity—

DUPRÉ. To insure for himself the possessions of the young Count, it was necessary that Mr. Darlemont should be able to announce his death and prove it in the court of justice. He was obliged to have two witnesses—the first was the host where we lodged at Paris, and whom he bribed with money—

ST. A. (laying his hand on Dupré's mouth). Wretch !—(then changing his tone) —Finish.

FRANVAL. And the second witness ?—

DUPRÉ. Was myself. (De l'Epée explains to Theodore the falsehood of which Dupré had been guilty, tracing some lines on his left hand with the forefinger of his right, and then bending his head with closed eyes on his right hand, thus expressing death. Theodore looks indignantly at Dupré, and draws back from him.)

Dupré (continues). Conducted into an office where everything had been prepared, I signed the certificate of the death of Julius Harancour, and a short time after we departed for Toulouse, where, to support this act, a monument of atrocious perfidy—

St. A. (in a most distressing tone). Stop!—It is no longer possible to doubt.—Oh! how overwhelming is the fearful weight of a father's crime! (He falls into a chair, supported by Franval, overcome with grief.)

Dupré. From that fatal day I have never found a moment's peace. God is just and has preserved this innocent victim; I am come to offer to make a public confession, and to denounce myself at the tribunal of justice. I know the severity of the penalty which awaits me; I am resigned to all: happy if in expiating the crime of which I was the accomplice, I can assist in repairing the evils it has caused.

St. A. (rising with determination, as if struck with an idea). Yes, yes, we must repair them—follow me, unhappy old man.

(He drags Dupré.)

Dupré. Dispose of me, Sir.

Franval (running after St. Alme and holding him). St. Alme, where are you going?

St. A. Where despair calls me.

De l'Epée. Consider that Theodore—

St. A. The sight of him increases my agony.

Franval. What do you mean to do?

St. A. Avenge him or die.

De l'Epée (holding him with Franval). Your reason wanders.

St. A. Release me!

Franval. Allow your friend—

St. A. (wildly tearing himself from the hands of De l'Epée and Franval). O father! father!—(to Franval and De l'Epe, who still try to hold him) Let me go! let me go!

(He goes out precipitately, taking Dupré.)

De l'Epée, by signs, re-assures Theodore, who is disturbed and agitated ; he also observes Clemence, who is in the deepest dejection.

Mrs. F.   At length we know all the plot carried out by this Darlemont.

Franval.   To take advantage of the infirmity of a defenceless, unprotected child ! To violate the rights of relationship and confidence ! I confess that I needed the testimony of this old man to make me believe such perfidy.

De l'Epée. You see Theodore was not mistaken.

Mrs. F. Do you still hesitate, my son, to deliver up this guilty man to the vengeance of the law ? Will you wait till he employ his credit and opulence to forestall your proceedings ?

De l'Epée.   I must add to these important remarks, that Theodore is not the only one to whom I owe my care ; my other pupils whom I left in Paris, suffer much from my absence, and I must for their sake economize my time.

Franval.   Yes, yes ; I should be culpable in delaying longer to fulfil the duty your confidence imposes on me.   Let us sign this deed. (De l'Epée and Theodore sign the writing which is upon the desk.)

Clemence (aside). There's no more hope, then ?
(Enter Dominic and Marianne.)

Mrs. F.   Ah !   Come in, Dominic, come in.— Well !   Do you bring us nobody ?

Dominic (still quite out of breath).   'Tis n't for want of having run and looked everywhere.—First, we went to the house of Peter, the old groom.—He had gone out early in the morning, with his wife.

Marianne.   From there we went to poor Maurice, the coachman's widow—

Dominic.   In the country for the day.—But we told several people, who live near, to tell them to come here as soon as they returned.

Franval.   You took especial care to conceal the motive ?

DOMINIC. My master knows well that when a secret is entrusted to me—

FRANVAL (holding the deed in one hand and taking his hat with the other). I have no doubt that this deed, from the nature of the facts which it contains, (to De l'Epée) and especially under a name like yours, will excite all the zeal of the magistrates. You will both accompany me. (To Mrs. F. and Clemence, whose agitation increases to the highest degree.) If St. Alme should return in our absence, calm him, I entreat you, especially you, dear sister,—repeat to him how much this pains me,—but a single instant of delay might injure the young Count, and give his oppressor fearful odds.—Let us go.

(A noise outside is heard.)

CLEMENCE. I hear some one, I think.

DOMINIC (looking out of the door). It is Mr. St. Alme.—In what trouble! Great God! what agitation!

(St. Alme, entering in haste, without hat or sword, and in the greatest excitement.)

ST. A. My friend! my friend! (He falls breathless into the arms of Franval, who places him in an easy chair. Theodore flies to his assistance, and shows intense interest. All the others surround them. After a little time, Theodore returns to his place, at the right hand of De l'Epée.)

FRANVAL. St. Alme, compose yourself.

ST. ALME (looking at those who surround him). My father, (he tries to continue, but emotion chokes his voice).

FRANVAL. Explain yourself.

ST. A. My father,—

DE L'EPÉE. Speak—tell all.

ST. A. (with broken voice, but gradually regaining strength). Made desperate by the recital of that old servant, (he rises) I rushed—I forced open the door of the room where my father had shut himself in. Dupré, who followed me,—

told him that he had confessed all to you,—and
that he was resolved to go and denounce him with
himself. — "You made me share your crime,"
added he, "I will make you share my punishment." Struck by the threat of the old man, my
father shuddered ;—I seized the moment, and with
the point of my sword on my breast, I said, in
my turn, "I am now to be dishonoured by your
crime; still young, I should have too long to
suffer,—therefore I die before your eyes,—if, this
instant, this very instant, you do not sign your
recognition of Julius Harancour." This cry of
despair, the idea of undying infamy, and above
all things the certainty of my death, at last pro-
duced the effect I expected. Nature triumphed,
my father yielded,—and, with a trembling hand,
he traced this writing which I bring you. (He
takes it from his bosom and gives it to Franval.)
There it is ! There it is !

FRANVAL (reading). "I recognize Julius Har-
cour in the pupil of Mr. De l'Epée, known by the
name of Theodore, and I am prepared to reinstate
him in his rights."

DE L'EPÉE (uncovering his head). Almighty
God ! thanks be to Thee, for ever. (He takes the
writing from the hand of Franval, and gives it to
Theodore.)

FRANVAL (to St. Alme). Of what a weight, my
friend, you have just relieved my heart ! (He tears
the accusation which he still holds in his hand.)

THEODORE, as soon as he has read the writing,
throws himself at the feet of De l'Epée, and kisses
them ; rises, and, transported with joy, runs to
throw himself on Franval's shoulder; then advances in front of St. Alme, looks at him and stops
suddenly as if struck by an idea, and darts to the
desk, where he traces a few lines at the bottom of
Darlemont's writing.

FRANVAL. What is he doing ? and what is his
intention ?

DE L'EPÉE. I know not.

ST. A. He appears peculiarly moved.

CLEMENCE. Tears are starting from his eyes.

THEODORE comes back to St. Alme, takes one of his hands, lays it on his heart, and with the other gives him the writing to read.

ST. A. (reading, in great emotion). "I cannot be happy at the expense of my first friend. I give him half of the wealth which is restored to me. He cannot refuse me this; we were always accustomed from infancy to share as brothers. On finding each other again our hearts must resume their former habits." My friend! (He and Theodore again mingle their caresses.)

DE L'EPÉE (pressing Theodore to his heart). This action alone repays me for all I have suffered for him.

MARIANNE. He will be as benevolent as his father. Sir, (to De l'Epée) may I hope to be allowed to end my days with my young master?

DE L'EPÉE. Yes, my good woman, you and all the old servants of the family you may find.

FRANVAL. But on this condition, Marianne, that you will, like ourselves, keep perfect silence as to the cause of the misfortunes of the young Count.

ST. A. Why can I not blot out such a remembrance?—and how shall I be able to endure its bitterness?

DE L'EPÉE. If Miss Clemence would help you—by sharing your fate?

FRANVAL (to De l'Epée). It is plain that nothing escapes your penetration.

Mrs. F. But think, only, that such a marriage—

DE L'EPÉE. Will fulfil the vows of two who love each other, and perfect the happiness which I desire to promote.

Mrs. F. You, Sir, alone, could gain my consent—how could such benevolence be resisted?

DE L'EPÉE (signs to Theodore, expressing marriage by twice joining his hands together, and pointing to the finger for the wedding-ring. Theodore joins the hands of St. Alme and Clemence, pressing them both together on his heart.)

DOMINIC (pointing to Theodore). Good young man! If he can express himself so well without speaking, what would he be if we could hear him speak?

CLEMENCE. Happy moment, which I was far from expecting!

ST. A. My happiness can be felt, but not expressed.

FRANVAL. My joy can only be equalled by my astonishment. (To De l'Epée)—Benevolent man, how proud must you be of your pupil! Compare what he is at this moment with what he was when first presented to you, and then enjoy your work.

DE L'EPÉE (looking at Theodore and those around him). At length I behold him restored to his home, crowned with the sacred name of his forefathers, and already surrounded by people whom he has rendered happy. O Providence! I have nothing more to desire in the world; and when I put off this mortal body, I shall be able to say, "Let me sleep in peace; I have finished my work."

THE END.

I. E. Chillcott, Steam Press, Bristol.